A FOLLETT BEGINNING-TO-READ BOOK

Miller

GLORIA D. MIKLOWITZ

BAREFOOT BOY

ILLUSTRATED BY JIM COLLINS

ISBN   0-695-30680-4   Paper Binding
ISBN   0-695-40680-9   Titan Binding

Follett Publishing Company   *Chicago*

Library of Congress Catalog Card Number: 64-21040

1011121314/80797877

Paul Steven was a happy boy.

He liked many things.

He liked to play with his brother
and run with his dog.

He liked to chase his cat.

He liked to climb trees and
jump fences.

But there was one thing
Paul Steven did not like.

There was one thing that
made him unhappy.

Paul Steven did not like
to wear shoes.

Paul Steven never did like
to wear shoes.

When he was five years old,
he did not like to wear shoes.

So he lost them.

He lost a pair of white shoes
and a pair of brown shoes.

He lost a pair of sneakers too.

"How did you lose your white shoes?"
his mother asked.

"I was playing in the sand,"
Paul Steven said.

"The sand felt good on my toes.
The river felt good too.

My white shoes fell in the river."

"How did you lose your brown shoes?"
his father asked.

"I had pebbles in my shoes,"
Paul Steven said.

"So I took them off and put them
in my pockets."

"The pebbles?" his father asked.

"The shoes," Paul Steven said.

"And then I climbed a tree.
I jumped a fence, and I chased a
cat," he said.

"You cannot climb high. You
cannot jump far. You cannot run fast
with shoes on, you know," Paul Steven
said to his father.

"Go on," his father said.

"My brown shoes fell out of my
pockets," Paul Steven said.

"How did you lose your sneakers?"
his mother and father asked.

They were very angry.

"I took them off to cross the
river," Paul Steven said.

"Then I heard a fire truck.
I ran to the fire.

When I came back, I could not
find my sneakers."

When Paul Steven was six years old,
he did not like to wear shoes.

But he did not lose his shoes,
and he did not lose his sneakers.

He did not lose them because he
stopped wearing them.

Paul Steven became an Indian.

"Shoes are fine for girls,"
Paul Steven said to his mother.

"Shoes are fine for boys.

Shoes are fine for mothers and
for fathers.

Shoes are even fine for horses.

But I never heard of an Indian
wearing shoes."

Sometimes Paul Steven was an Indian brave.

Barefoot, he would stalk the paleface mailman from door to door.

Sometimes Paul Steven was an Indian guide.

Barefoot, he would lead the paleface settlers to the river.

Sometimes Paul Steven was an
Indian chief.

Barefoot, he would pass his
peace pipe from brave to brave.

And sometimes Paul Steven was
a wild Indian.

Barefoot, he would run and shout
and shake his tomahawk.

"Listen, Paul Steven,"
his mother said.

"Being an Indian brave is fine.
Being an Indian guide or an Indian chief
is fine too. Even being a wild Indian
is fine."

His father said, "But going without
shoes all the time is not fine!"

Paul Steven sat as an Indian sits.

He put down his peace pipe.

He put down his tomahawk.

He crossed his arms.

And he listened.

"Even Indians know that
pebbles hurt," his mother said.
"And bees sting.
And thorns bite.
And glass cuts.

Even Indians know
the ground is cold in winter.
And hot in summer!"

And his father said,

"Even wild Indians wear shoes.
They wear moccasins.

Sometimes in summer they go
barefoot.

But winter is cold.

In winter even wild Indians
wear moccasins.

Where are your moccasins,
Paul Steven?"

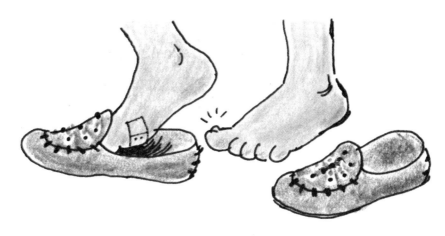

Paul Steven took his moccasins from his pockets.

He put one moccasin on his right foot.

He put it on over an old cut on his foot.

He put one moccasin on his left foot.

He put it on over the bee sting on his toe.

His mother said,

"When you were five years old,
you lost all your shoes.

When you were six years old,
you would not wear your shoes.

Tomorrow is your birthday.
You will be seven.

Tomorrow, will you wear shoes?"

On his birthday Paul Steven
got many presents.

From his grandmother,
he got a cowboy suit.

From his grandfather,
he got a cowboy hat.

From his brother,
he got a gun.

But from his mother and father,
he got the best present of all.

He got a pair of high, shiny
COWBOY BOOTS.

Paul Steven was very happy to
be seven years old.

He put on the cowboy suit from
his grandmother.

He put on the cowboy hat from
his grandfather.

He put on the gun from
his brother.

And last of all, he put on the
new pair of high, shiny cowboy boots.

"How long will those boots
stay on, Paul Steven?" his mother asked.

Paul Steven felt his new hat.

He flipped his new gun.

He rubbed his new boots on the
legs of his new suit.

"They will stay on," Paul Steven said. "I might take off my shoes, and I might take off my sneakers.

But a cowboy never takes off his boots.

A cowboy even SLEEPS with his boots on!"

BAREFOOT BOY

Reading Level: Level Two. *Barefoot Boy* has a total vocabulary of 183 words. It has been tested in beginning second grade classes, where it was read with ease.

Uses of this Book: Reading for fun. Paul Steven was a problem to his parents because he would not wear shoes. Everyone will enjoy this charming and amusing story, especially the logical way the "barefoot boy problem" is finally solved.

Word List

All of the 183 words used in *Barefoot Boy* are listed. Regular plurals *(-s)* and regular verb forms *(-s, -ed, -ing)* of words already on the list are not listed separately, but the endings are given in parentheses after the word.

5 Paul	his	did	so
Steven	brother	not	lost
was	run	that	them
a	dog	made	pair
happy	chase (d)	him	of
boy (s)	cat	unhappy	white
he	climb (ed)	wear (ing)	brown
like (d)	tree (s)	shoes	sneakers
many	jump (ed)	7 never	too
thing (s)	fence (s)	when	8 how
to	6 but	five	you
play (ing)	there	years	lose
with	one	old	your

mother (s)
asked
I
in
the
sand
said
felt
good
on
my
toe (s)
river
fell
9 father (s)
had
pebbles
took
off
and
put
pockets
10 then
cannot
high
far
fast
know
go (ing)
out
11 they
were
very

angry
cross (ed)
heard
fire
truck
ran
came
back
could
find
12 six
because
stopped
became
an
Indian (s)
13 are
fine
for
girls
even
horses
14 sometimes
brave
barefoot
would
stalk
paleface
mailman
from
door
15 guide
lead

settlers
16 chief
pass
peace
pipe
17 wild
shout
shake
tomahawk
18 listen (ed)
be (ing)
is
without
all
time
19 sat
as
sits
down
arms
20 hurt
bee (s)
sting
thorns
bite
glass
cut (s)
21 ground
cold
winter
hot
summer
22 moccasin (s)

where
23 right
foot
it
over
left
24 tomorrow
birthday
will
seven
25 got
present (s)
grandmother
cowboy
suit
grandfather
hat
gun
26 best
shiny
boots
last
new
28 long
those
stay
flipped
rubbed
legs
29 might
take (s)
sleeps

The Follett BEGINNING-TO-READ Books

Purpose of the Beginning-to-Read Books: To provide easy-to-read materials that will appeal to the interests of primary children. Careful attention is given to vocabulary load and sentence length, but the first criterion is interest to children.

Reading Levels: These books are written at three reading levels, indicated by one, two, or three dots beneath the *Beginning-to-Read* symbol on the back cover. *Level One* books can be read by first grade children in the last half of the school year. As children increase their reading ability they will be able to enjoy *Level Two* books. And as they grow further in their reading ability they will progress to *Level Three* books. Some first grade children will read *Level Two* and *Level Three* books. Many third graders, and even some fourth graders, will read and enjoy *Level One* and *Level Two* books, as well as *Level Three* books. The range of interest of *Beginning-to-Read* books stretches far beyond their reading level.

Use of the Beginning-to-Read Books: Because of their high interest and readability, these books are ideal for independent reading by primary children—at school, in the library, and at home. The books may also be incorporated into the basic reading program to develop children's interests, expand their vocabularies, and improve word-attack skills. It has been suggested that they might serve as the foundation for a skillfully directed reading program. Many *Beginning-to-Read* books correlate with the social studies, science, and other subject fields. All will help children grow in the language arts. Children will read the *Beginning-to-Read* books with confidence, with success, and with real enjoyment.